BUZZSPINN

The guardian veil

Copyright © 2024 by Buzzspinn

All rights reserved. No part of this publication may be reproduced, stored or transmitted in any form or by any means, electronic, mechanical, photocopying, recording, scanning, or otherwise without written permission from the publisher. It is illegal to copy this book, post it to a website, or distribute it by any other means without permission.

This novel is entirely a work of fiction. The names, characters and incidents portrayed in it are the work of the author's imagination. Any resemblance to actual persons, living or dead, events or localities is entirely coincidental.

First edition

This book was professionally typeset on Reedsy. Find out more at reedsy.com

Contents

1	Chapter 1	1
2	Chapter 2	5
3	Chapter 3	13
4	Chapter 4	23
5	Chapter 5	29
6	Chapter 6	38
7	Chapter 7	43
8	Chapter 8	56
9	Chapter 9	64
10	Chapter 10	69
11	Chapter 11	75

One

Chapter 1

Evelyn woke with a jolt, the remnants of a fleeting dream slipping through her mind like shadows retreating from the dawn. The clock on her bedside table read 5:47 a.m., its soft glow piercing the dim haze of early morning. For a moment, she lay still, uncertain of where she was, as if caught between the fading grasp of the dream and the weight of reality.

Her eyes adjusted to the familiar confines of her small apartment in Eldoria. The golden light of morning spilled through the blinds, painting streaks across the worn wooden floor. Outside, the city murmured to life, its distant hum reaching her ears like the first notes of a waking symphony.

Evelyn sighed, stretching limbs heavy with reluctance. Each movement felt tethered to the mundanity of her existence, her body protesting the early hour as if it knew today would demand more than routine. Yet, nothing in the apartment

The guardian veil

betrayed the day as anything but ordinary. Her bookshelves leaned under the weight of old texts, the air carried the faint scent of parchment and dust, and the kettle sat ready on the counter, waiting to fulfill its daily ritual.

But something lingered. A whisper, faint and fleeting, stirred in the back of her mind—a sensation not wholly unfamiliar, yet impossible to place. She dismissed it as she always had, shaking off the feeling with the practiced ease of someone used to ignoring the intangible.

Still, as she rose from her bed, her feet touching the cool floor, Evelyn couldn't help but feel it again. A pulse. A murmur. Something was different, though the world around her seemed to insist otherwise.

Eldoria was a city of contrasts, where the ancient and modern coexisted in an uneasy balance.

Its skyline stretched boldly into the heavens, a jagged silhouette of gleaming towers and weathered stone facades. Streets twisted like rivers through its bustling heart, lined with market stalls spilling over with wares both exotic and mundane. The scent of roasted chestnuts mingled with the tang of oil from food carts, while above it all, the sharp cries of street vendors competed with the endless hum of traffic.

The weather in Eldoria seemed to reflect its spirit: unpredictable, with moments of bright sunshine quickly giving way to sudden rain. And yet, on days like today, the air carried a curious stillness, as though the city itself were pausing to draw a breath before another surge of motion.

Its people were as varied as its streets: merchants haggling over prices with voices honed sharp from practice, musicians playing lilting tunes on street corners, and scholars clutching their books as they hurried through the chaos. Eldoria's soul

Chapter 1

was a blend of progress and tradition, a place where one might find a tech-savvy inventor tinkering with the latest gadget beside an herbalist who swore by remedies passed down through the ages.

Beliefs ran deep here, though not always uniform. Some worshipped the old gods whose stories were carved into the foundations of the city itself. Others placed their faith in logic, in the unyielding precision of science. And then there were those who believed in nothing but Eldoria itself, their conviction rooted in the ceaseless rhythm of its streets and the unspoken promise of opportunity.

For Evelyn, however, Eldoria's vitality was best observed from a safe distance. Her haven lay within the city library, a towering sanctuary of stone and glass that seemed as old as the city itself. Inside, the chaos of Eldoria melted away into a realm of hushed whispers and soft, deliberate footsteps. Here, surrounded by shelves sagging under the weight of forgotten stories, she found her peace.

The routine of cataloging ancient texts was far from glamorous, but Evelyn had developed a fondness for the predictable rhythm of her work. She often joked that the books were better conversationalists than the people outside—at least they didn't interrupt. Besides, the smell of old parchment and ink was oddly comforting, even if it did make her sneeze on occasion.

Her favorite part of the job? The oddities. Every so often, she'd stumble across a book with missing pages, strange annotations, or drawings that defied explanation. Once, she'd found a recipe for "Dragon's Breath Stew" tucked between the pages of a history of Eldoria. She'd kept that one for herself, though she had yet to find a dragon willing to donate its breath.

Yet, even in the stillness of the library, there were times when

The guardian veil

an odd feeling would stir within her—when the air seemed to hum faintly, and the ancient books felt alive, as if sharing secrets meant for no one else.

She always brushed it off as her imagination.

But today, as Evelyn sat on the edge of her bed, the feeling was different—more persistent, more vivid. The faint hum that usually faded with the remnants of her dreams seemed to linger in the air, vibrating softly against her senses. It wasn't just a fleeting sensation now; it felt alive, like the murmur of distant voices just out of reach.

The whispers, if they could even be called that, seemed to gather in the corners of her room, threading through the golden morning light streaming in through the blinds. They weren't words she could understand, yet they carried a weight, an urgency, that made her heart quicken. It was as though the air itself had shifted, thick with something unseen and waiting.

She rubbed her temples and shook her head, willing the strange feeling to fade, but it clung to her like the last threads of a dream refusing to let go.

Two

Chapter 2

Evelyn had never been a morning person, and today proved no exception. Forcing herself out of bed had been nothing short of a heroic act. She'd flopped back onto the mattress twice, stared at the ceiling in protest for at least five minutes, and even briefly considered calling in sick just to avoid whatever odd energy had unsettled her earlier. Eventually, sheer guilt—and a strong desire to avoid the judgmental stares of her boss—won out.

Dragging herself out the door hadn't been much easier. Her jacket was buttoned wrong, she realized halfway down the block, and she was still wearing mismatched socks, one bearing a cheerful pineapple and the other, a solemn, lonely stripe. "Perfectly balanced," she muttered to herself, "like my life."

By the time she reached the library, her grogginess had faded, but the strange feeling that had plagued her morning remained.

The library greeted her with its familiar quiet, the scent of old paper and polished wood offering its usual comfort. Yet, as she stepped through the aisles of towering oak shelves, something felt... off. The dusty tomes, worn and faded from centuries of handling, had always commanded her respect, if not outright awe. Today, though, they seemed different.

It wasn't a dramatic change—no glowing lights or ominous music—but the air felt heavier, charged, as though the books themselves were alive with some unseen energy. She paused, running her fingers lightly over the spines of a few volumes. Each touch sent a faint tingle through her fingertips, like brushing against static electricity.

"Okay," she whispered to herself, "either I'm sleep-deprived, or I've walked into a bad paranormal movie."

Shaking her head, Evelyn descended the staircase that led to the library's archives. This was her favorite part of the building, a secluded haven of rare manuscripts and forgotten treasures. Down here, the bustle of the city above seemed a world away, replaced by the hushed reverence of history.

As her eyes adjusted to the dim light, one book caught her attention. It rested on a lower shelf, slightly out of place, its leather binding shimmering faintly as though dust refused to cling to it. A thin silver thread ran along its spine, glinting like a strand of moonlight in the shadowy corner.

Evelyn hesitated. The book seemed... alive, its presence almost daring her to reach for it. "Well," she muttered, crouching down, "if this is cursed, at least my pineapple sock will distract the demons."

Her hand hovered for a moment, fingers trembling slightly, before she finally touched the cover. A jolt of warmth spread through her hand, startling her enough to let out a small gasp. The hum she had felt earlier that morning returned, sharper

Chapter 2

now, resonating in the quiet space around her.

She took a deep breath, her heart pounding. Whatever this book was, it had waited long enough.

With a steadying breath, Evelyn opened the book, its old leather cover creaking faintly in protest. The pages within seemed almost alive, their surface etched with intricate illustrations of worlds she could hardly begin to comprehend. Towers of light that reached into endless skies, rivers that shimmered like liquid starlight, and figures half-glimpsed in swirling clouds.

The text was no less strange. The words seemed to writhe as if unwilling to be confined by the page, their shapes shifting, revealing meanings that danced just out of reach. They stirred something in her—an odd familiarity, as though she had once known these ideas in another lifetime, only to forget them until now.

As her eyes roamed the pages, a door seemed to unfasten within her mind, a latch undone by the sheer weight of the book's secrets. Her breath quickened, and the room around her faded, dissolving into a realm that bloomed like a dream made real.

Colors erupted around her, more vivid than anything she'd ever seen. A vast sky stretched endlessly above, its hues shifting from gold to violet in a mesmerizing cascade. Ethereal beings, their forms shimmering with unearthly grace, drifted among the clouds as though the air itself carried them.

For a moment, Evelyn felt as though she were soaring alongside them, her heart lifted by an overwhelming sense of freedom, weightless and unbound. But just as quickly, the scene shifted. At the edges of the vibrant world, the light dimmed, and shadows gathered.

The guardian veil

They were shapes without form, dark figures moving in unnatural ways, their presence suffocating and cold. Though they kept their distance, Evelyn could feel their attention, sharp and unrelenting, fixed on her. They didn't advance, but they didn't need to. The very sight of them was enough to make her heart pound.

"Who are you?" she whispered, though she wasn't certain she wanted to know the answer.

The shadows seemed to ripple, as if mocking her fear. The light around her began to dim further, the vibrant colors retreating into gray. And just as the tension reached its peak, a voice—soft but firm—broke through the vision.

"Evelyn."

She jolted, her surroundings snapping back into focus. The library's dimly lit archive came rushing back, and she realized she was clutching the book so tightly her fingers ached. The whispers in the air, once faint and distant, now felt louder, pressing in on her from all sides.

Whatever she had just seen wasn't just a trick of her imagination. The book held something far greater—and far more dangerous—than she could have ever anticipated.

Evelyn slammed the book shut, her heart hammering as though it were trying to escape her chest. The whispers that had seemed distant now pressed in close, curling around her like an unseen mist. Her hands trembled as she clutched the book to her chest, its strange warmth seeping through her blouse. She cast a frantic glance around the dim archive, half-expecting those shadowy figures from her vision to emerge from the gloom.

The library's usual stillness felt oppressive now, the silence broken only by the faint hum of the overhead lights and the

Chapter 2

erratic rhythm of her own breathing. She tried to ground herself, forcing deep breaths, but the weight of what she had seen refused to loosen its grip.

"This is insane," she muttered under her breath, as if hearing her own voice would somehow restore normalcy. But the book in her arms was real, its weight anchoring her to the strange reality she'd just glimpsed. She needed to leave—now.

Evelyn tucked the book under her arm, its smooth cover oddly comforting despite the storm of questions raging in her mind. She peeked over her shoulder as she climbed the stairs back to the main floor, her footsteps echoing louder than they should have. It was just the library, she told herself. Just a building filled with books and silence. But each shadow she passed seemed darker, each corner sharper, and she couldn't shake the feeling that someone—or something—was watching.

The moment she stepped outside, the cool evening air hit her like a balm, dispelling the lingering tension. The streetlights flickered to life, their glow casting long shadows across the pavement as Evelyn hurried home. She couldn't quite put into words what had happened, but she knew one thing: she wasn't leaving this mystery behind.

—-

As Evelyn stepped into her apartment, the sound of the door closing was met with a delighted chirp, followed by the unmistakable patter of tiny paws. Her cat, Nimbus, bounded toward her with all the energy of a small storm. A fluffy gray ball of mischief, Nimbus had eyes like molten gold and a tail that seemed perpetually in motion, waving like a feather duster on a mission.

"Hey, buddy," Evelyn murmured, bending down to scratch behind his ears. Nimbus immediately leaned into her hand,

The guardian veil

purring loudly enough to rival a coffee grinder. His enthusiasm was infectious, and Evelyn couldn't help but smile despite the tension still knotting her chest.

Nimbus, however, was not one to linger on formalities. In a flash, he darted between her legs, rubbing against her ankles before launching himself onto the couch. He flopped onto his back, paws in the air, staring at her with an expectant look. Evelyn shook her head. "You're ridiculous, you know that?"

Nimbus answered by rolling dramatically onto his side, batting at an invisible foe before leaping to his feet and chasing his own tail in dizzying circles. Evelyn couldn't help but laugh, the sound breaking through the lingering unease from the library. "Alright, alright, I'll play later. Promise."

Nimbus followed her as she moved to the dining table, leaping gracefully onto a nearby chair. He watched her with unblinking intensity as she placed the book down, his tail flicking in time with her movements. It wasn't often he stayed still for long, but tonight, it was as if he sensed something unusual.

That evening, Evelyn sat at her small dining table, the book laid out before her like an offering. Nimbus perched nearby, his usual playful energy replaced with a quiet curiosity, his golden eyes fixed on the glowing pages. The comfort of her apartment did little to soothe her nerves. The warm light from the lamp overhead should have softened the tension, but instead, it cast her shadow long and distorted against the walls. Even Nimbus's presence, typically a source of grounding comfort, couldn't dispel the strange heaviness in the air.

Nimbus pawed at the table, his claws tapping softly against the wood, but even his antics couldn't pull her focus away from the book. The symbols shimmered faintly, their light dancing across the room. Nimbus gave a soft meow, as if to remind her

Chapter 2

he was still there, and Evelyn reached out absently to scratch his head. "Don't worry, Nim," she whispered, though she wasn't sure who she was trying to reassure more—her cat or herself.

Her fingers traced the strange symbols etched into the book's pages. They felt almost alive under her touch, their texture shifting slightly, as if responding to her curiosity. A faint light began to glow from the text, soft and otherworldly, spreading across the room.

The shadows around her flickered, twisting unnaturally in the pale glow. Evelyn froze, her breath caught in her throat. It wasn't just the symbols pulling her in now—it was the very air around her, tugging her forward with an almost physical force.

Her heart raced, but she couldn't pull away. The book, with its unearthly light and enigmatic pull, seemed to hold all the answers she sought—and all the danger she feared.

"Stop, you cannot!" Evelyn whispered to herself, her voice shaky as if the words alone could anchor her to reality. But even as the warning escaped her lips, she knew it was futile. The pull of the book was undeniable, a magnetic force that both terrified and intrigued her.

The air thickened around her, heavy and electric, vibrating with an energy that made the hairs on her arms stand on end. Nimbus, sensing the shift, leapt from the chair to the floor, his tail puffed up like a bottlebrush. He hissed softly, a low sound of warning, before retreating to the far corner of the room, his golden eyes wide with alarm.

Evelyn's gaze snapped back to the book as a swirling mist began to rise from its pages, forming a vortex of shimmering light above the table. Colors she couldn't name spun and twisted, their brilliance dazzling yet unnerving. It wasn't just light—it was alive, pulsating with a rhythm that seemed to

The guardian veil

match the racing of her heart.

"Come see," whispered the voice again, soft and melodic, yet carrying a weight that made her knees weak.

She hesitated, her trembling hands hovering above the book. Fear coursed through her veins, cold and sharp, but it was met with an equal measure of something else: curiosity. A yearning for answers, for understanding, burned within her, refusing to be ignored.

With a deep breath, Evelyn pressed her palm onto the glowing pages. The moment her skin touched the text, a surge of warmth flooded her body, spreading from her fingertips to her core. The light flared, blinding and all-encompassing, erasing the room around her.

She felt weightless, untethered, as though she had been plucked from her reality and cast adrift in a sea of endless possibility. The faint hum that had followed her all day grew into a crescendo, surrounding her, consuming her.

Three

Chapter 3

When the light receded, Evelyn staggered, her breath catching in her throat. She was no longer in her apartment; the familiar walls and furniture had vanished, replaced by an otherworldly landscape that defied comprehension.

Beneath her feet, the ground shimmered, a translucent surface that pulsed with energy in time with her heartbeat. It was like walking on liquid glass, yet it held firm, shifting slightly underfoot as though alive. Above her, the sky swirled with impossibly vibrant hues—ribbons of gold, violet, and deep blue twisting together in a kaleidoscope of motion. Clouds, if they could be called that, drifted lazily, their forms fluid and luminous, like glowing rivers suspended in the air.

Evelyn turned in a slow circle, trying to take in the vastness of the realm. She had no words to describe it, no point of reference in her mind to understand what she was seeing. A

The guardian veil

mix of exhilaration and dread coursed through her veins, her pulse racing.

"Is this real?" she breathed, her voice barely above a whisper. The question lingered in the stillness, unanswered.

As she took a hesitant step forward, a low hum filled the air, growing louder, deeper, vibrating through her chest. She froze, her breath catching again as a figure began to take shape in the fog that hung on the edges of the horizon.

It moved with a fluid grace, emerging from the mist like a wraith stepping out of shadow. Tall and radiant, the being seemed to glow from within, its light soft yet piercing. Its wings—if that's what they were—unfurled like great plumes of luminescent feathers, extending far beyond what should have been possible.

Evelyn felt a shiver run down her spine as the figure drew closer, its presence both mesmerizing and overwhelming. She didn't know whether to step back or stand her ground.

"Welcome, Evelyn," the being said, its voice rich and melodic, echoing as though the words were carried on the wind.

She swallowed hard, her throat dry. "Who… who are you?" she asked, her voice shaking despite her attempt to sound steady.

The figure stopped a few feet away, its radiant form somehow both comforting and intimidating. "I am Liora," it replied, the name carrying a weight that settled in her chest. "A Guardian of the Realms."

Evelyn's brow furrowed, her mind racing to piece together what little sense she could make of this. "Guardian? Guardian of what?"

"The balance between worlds," Liora said, gliding closer. Its wings shimmered as they folded neatly behind it, the light

Chapter 3

refracting like a thousand tiny prisms. "You possess a unique spark, Evelyn—a rare connection that has brought you here, across the threshold between realms. But with that connection comes great peril."

Evelyn felt her legs weaken, though she remained upright. "Peril? What kind of peril?"

Liora's gaze, though not human, felt impossibly knowing, like it could see into the depths of her thoughts. "There are those who dwell in shadow, who seek to exploit your awareness and fracture the boundaries of your world. They are drawn to your light, and they will stop at nothing to extinguish it."

The vibrant colors of the landscape seemed to dim slightly at Liora's words, and Evelyn felt the weight of them settle over her like a heavy cloak. "Why me?" she whispered, the question trembling on her lips.

"You were chosen, though not by design," Liora said, its voice softening. "The journey ahead will test you, but you are not without strength. You must decide whether to embrace your spark or allow it to fade."

Evelyn stared at the Guardian, her thoughts a whirlwind of fear and determination. The ground beneath her pulsed once more, as if urging her forward. Despite the uncertainty, she knew one thing: there was no turning back.

"What do I need to do?" she asked, her voice stronger now, though her hands still trembled at her sides.

Liora extended a glowing hand, gesturing toward the distant horizon where the mist seemed to part, revealing a faint, glimmering path. "Follow where the light guides you. Your journey has only just begun."

As Evelyn stepped forward, a strange, tingling warmth coursed through her body, starting in her feet and radiating upward with each step. The landscape seemed alive, shifting and morphing subtly as if the world itself responded to her presence. At first glance, it was beautiful—a realm that felt oddly familiar, as though it had been stitched together from fragments of her dreams. But the details revealed a reality beyond human comprehension.

To her left, fields of golden grass stretched endlessly, each blade catching the light and shimmering like spun glass. The air above the fields was alive with faint wisps of energy, floating lazily like dandelion seeds carried on an unseen breeze. Beyond the fields, mountains rose in the distance, their jagged peaks not gray but a deep, glowing sapphire, veined with rivers of molten gold.

To her right, an ocean spread out, vast and otherworldly, its surface rippling with impossible colors—shades of blue and green that seemed to pulse and shift, interwoven with streaks of crimson and silver. The waves didn't crash; they moved deliberately, as though aware of their own rhythm. In the depths, shadows of enormous creatures moved gracefully, their forms indistinct but their size unmistakable.

Overhead, the sky was unlike anything Evelyn had ever seen. It wasn't just a vast expanse of blue but a tapestry of light and motion. Hues of violet and gold swirled together, interspersed with streaks of bright white that crackled faintly like distant lightning. Stars—if that's what they were—hung low, so luminous that Evelyn could make out their faint flickers even in the daylight.

As she continued, the ground beneath her shifted with each step. Sometimes it felt soft, like stepping on clouds, and at other times firm and steady, resembling polished stone. The texture changed too, ranging from smooth to faintly prickly, like the

Chapter 3

surface itself was testing her resolve.

"Where are we headed?" she asked, her voice small against the vastness around her. Her eyes darted between the beauty and strangeness of the world, her awe mingling with an undercurrent of fear.

"To the Chamber of Unity," Liora responded, its voice serene yet resolute. "There, you will meet the Guardians who oversee the balance of all realms. They will enlighten you on the stakes of your journey."

Evelyn squinted toward the horizon. It seemed impossibly distant, but as she walked, the air ahead shimmered, and a structure began to emerge, faint at first, then solidifying with each step. It was unlike anything she had seen before—a towering spire of crystal and stone, its surface radiating soft light that danced like ripples on water.

The Chamber of Unity seemed to defy the laws of physics. Its base was impossibly narrow for something so massive, and its walls appeared translucent, yet within them, Evelyn could see faint figures moving—shapes of varying sizes, glowing softly. The structure pulsed naturally, as though it was alive, breathing in harmony with the world around it.

Evelyn felt her legs slow as she approached, her apprehension growing. The weight of Liora's words pressed down on her now. She didn't fully understand what awaited her, but she could feel its importance in her bones.

The energy around her grew stronger, vibrating in the air and thrumming in her chest. She swallowed hard, her steps faltering for just a moment. "Will they—" she hesitated, glancing at Liora. "Will they even want to see me?"

"They already see you," Liora replied, gliding beside her. Its wings shimmered as it gestured toward the towering structure.

The guardian veil

"You were always meant to arrive here, Evelyn. The Guardians have been waiting."

The path ahead shimmered, leading directly to the Chamber's entrance, its grand doors carved with symbols that seemed to glow and shift as Evelyn drew closer.

Inside the chamber, Evelyn found herself standing before six figures, each unlike anything she had ever imagined. The Guardians, as Liora had called them, radiated an otherworldly presence that was both awe-inspiring and intimidating.

The **Guardian of Time** stood at the center, cloaked in flowing robes that seemed to shimmer with the colors of a thousand sunsets. His face was lined with the wisdom of countless ages, his eyes deep and penetrating, as though he could see not just Evelyn's present but her past and future as well. A faint golden clockwork halo spun slowly behind him, ticking softly in the silence.

To his left was the **Guardian of Nature**, her form almost blending with the chamber itself. Her skin was a mosaic of bark and leaves, and her hair flowed like a waterfall of ivy. Flowers bloomed and withered across her body in an endless cycle, and the air around her smelled of fresh earth and rain.

Beside her stood the **Guardian of Light**, who shone so brightly that Evelyn had to squint to take in her form. She seemed to be made entirely of pure, radiant energy, her edges blurring into the air around her. Her voice, when she spoke, carried the warmth of the morning sun.

On the other side of the Guardian of Time stood the **Guardian of Darkness**, a shadowy figure cloaked in a deep black mist. His eyes glowed faintly like embers, and his voice was low and resonant, like the distant rumble of a storm. Though intimidating, there was a strange calmness about him,

Chapter 3

as if he carried secrets only the brave dared to uncover.

The **Guardian of Space** was next, her body a swirling galaxy of stars and constellations. She floated a few inches above the ground, her form constantly shifting, her voice echoing as though it came from the farthest reaches of the cosmos.

Finally, the **Guardian of Knowledge** stood tall and steady, his body appearing as a shimmering library of books and scrolls. Pages of ancient texts moved across his surface, and his voice carried the weight of millennia, measured and deliberate.

The Guardians watched Evelyn with expressions that ranged from curiosity to quiet expectation. She felt the weight of their collective gaze pressing on her, yet she held her ground, determined to understand why she had been brought here.

"As an unwitting traveler between dimensions, you have set a ripple in motion," the Guardian of Time said, his voice smooth but grave. "Each choice you make will carry consequences that resonate far beyond your world. You must tread carefully."

Evelyn nodded, her throat dry. "I understand. But what are the rules I need to follow?" she asked, her voice steady despite the nervous energy buzzing within her.

The Guardian of Nature stepped forward, her movements graceful, almost fluid. "First, you must respect the boundaries," she said, her voice as soft as a breeze but carrying an undeniable strength. "Crossing into another realm is not without cost. Every step you take beyond your world leaves a mark, and not all marks can be erased."

Evelyn swallowed hard, the weight of her actions settling heavily on her.

"Second," the Guardian of Space added, her voice echoing with infinite depth, "be mindful of your intentions. Curiosity is a double-edged sword. It can lead to discovery but also to destruction if wielded without care."

Evelyn felt the weight of the moment pressing on her, heavy and unrelenting. She hadn't asked for this—hadn't chosen to stumble into a world of Guardians and dimensions—but there was no denying the fire kindling in her chest. A quiet determination bloomed, fed by both fear and an unshakable resolve.

"I want to protect my realm," she said, her voice steady despite the storm of emotions swirling within her. "What can I do?"

The Guardians exchanged glances, their expressions grave yet tinged with something Evelyn couldn't quite place—understanding, perhaps, or a quiet acknowledgment of her courage.

"There is a disturbance," the Guardian of Darkness said at last, stepping forward. His shadowy form seemed to grow larger, the mist surrounding him swirling ominously. "Entities from beyond the Veil are drawn to your light. They sense your connection and seek to exploit it."

Evelyn felt a chill creep up her spine. "What do they want?" she asked, her voice barely above a whisper.

"To consume the essence of your reality," the Guardian of Light replied, her radiant presence dimming slightly as she spoke. "They thrive on the chaos and energy created by broken boundaries. If the Veil falls, your world and countless others will be at their mercy."

Evelyn swallowed hard, her mind racing. The word *consume* echoed in her thoughts, cold and relentless. "How can I stop them?"

"You must fortify the Veil," the Guardian of Knowledge said, his voice deliberate and measured. "It is the barrier that protects your world from the forces that would unravel it. But first, you

Chapter 3

must learn to harness the power within you."

Evelyn's heart pounded, but she nodded. "How do I do that?"

Liora stepped forward, her wings shimmering softly in the chamber's ethereal light. "Your journey begins now," she said, her voice both soothing and resolute. "You must venture into other realms to gather the Aetheric Seeds—fragments of pure energy that sustain the balance between dimensions. These seeds are the key to strengthening the Veil."

"Aetheric Seeds?" Evelyn repeated, the term both unfamiliar and daunting.

"They are the essence of creation," the Guardian of Nature explained, her voice like a rustling forest. "Each seed holds the power of its realm, a piece of the whole that sustains the balance of existence. They are scattered across the dimensions, hidden in places of great significance."

Evelyn glanced at each Guardian in turn, their forms towering and otherworldly, yet their words carried the weight of trust. "And I have to gather these seeds?" she asked.

"You must," the Guardian of Space confirmed. "But it will not be easy. Each realm you enter will test you, and each seed will demand a sacrifice. Only through perseverance and understanding can you succeed."

Evelyn took a deep breath, steadying herself. She didn't fully understand what lay ahead, but she knew she couldn't turn away now. "I'll do it," she said firmly. "I'll gather the seeds and protect the Veil."

The chamber seemed to brighten slightly, as if her resolve had shifted the very energy of the space.

"Then prepare yourself," Liora said, her wings unfurling slightly. "Your journey will take you far beyond anything you've known. Trust in your strength, and remember—you are never truly alone."

Evelyn felt a mix of fear and determination swirling within her, but she met Liora's gaze and nodded. Whatever challenges awaited her, she was ready to face them.

Four

Chapter 4

Evelyn's journey began with an uneasy resolve, her path shaped by the guidance of the mysterious Guardians. Her first destination was the Realm of Echoes, a strange and otherworldly place that felt like stepping into a dream where the past and present blurred together.

The air here shimmered with an ethereal haze, heavy with the weight of lives long past. As Evelyn moved cautiously forward, she saw the outlines of figures materializing around her—shimmering silhouettes that glowed faintly, their forms shifting and incomplete, as though they were only fragments of memories.

The voices came next, soft and mournful, like a thousand whispers carried on an invisible wind. Words blurred together in a symphony of regret, hope, and longing. They told no coherent story, yet each phrase struck a chord deep within Evelyn, as if the echoes knew her better than she knew herself.

The guardian veil

Her attention was drawn to a glowing figure ahead, smaller than the others. A little girl emerged from the haze, her outline flickering like a fragile candle. Her bright eyes glimmered with a strange mix of innocence and sorrow, a reflection of what had been lost.

"I was once whole," the girl whispered, her voice light yet haunting. As Evelyn stepped closer, a vivid memory flared to life around the child—a quaint village bathed in golden sunlight, its streets bustling with laughter and warmth. But just as quickly, the image dissolved, replaced by shadows and an empty void.

"Now I am a fragment, trapped in this realm." The girl's voice trembled with a quiet despair.

Evelyn crouched slightly to meet the girl's gaze, her heart tightening. "Why?" she asked softly, unable to look away from the child's piercing eyes.

The girl's form flickered, her features blurring momentarily before settling again. "Because I ignored the rules," she said, her tone heavy with regret. "I sought knowledge without understanding, reached for power I wasn't ready to wield, and paid the price. My actions unraveled the threads of my own existence."

The weight of her words hung in the air, pressing down on Evelyn like a tangible force. She thought of the warnings from the Guardians—the consequences of tampering with forces beyond her comprehension.

"Do not succumb to your temptations," the girl whispered, her voice a plea as much as a warning. "The echoes here are reminders—fragments of those who strayed too far."

Moved by the child's sorrow, Evelyn nodded solemnly. "I will heed your warning," she said, her voice steady.

Chapter 4

The girl's form flickered again, her edges dissolving into the swirling haze. "Then go," she said, her voice fading. "Do not linger here longer than you must."

—

After gathering the first Aetheric Seed—its glow reminiscent of the book that had first drawn her into this strange world—Evelyn pressed onward, feeling the weight of her mission settle deeper into her soul. The seed pulsed gently in her hand, a reminder of the fragile balance she was trying to protect.

Without hesitation, Evelyn began to transform her essence, allowing herself to slip beyond the boundaries of the familiar. She had learned from the Guardians how to weave through the unseen dimensions, but the experience was unlike anything she had ever imagined. With each step, she felt herself stretch beyond the limits of her own body, her consciousness expanding and melding with the very fabric of the multiverse.

The world around her rippled and shimmered, a series of possibilities unfolding before her eyes. The air was thick with energy, and the boundaries of reality seemed to warp and bend with her every movement.

In one realm, she encountered entities of such beauty that her breath caught in her chest. Ethereal beings with translucent wings that sparkled like starlight, their forms shifting like liquid light, their eyes deep with ancient wisdom. They welcomed her with silent grace, their presence calming yet strangely distant. They seemed to know her, to recognize the spark within her, but offered no words—only a quiet reverence for her journey.

But not all the realms were so serene. In others, darkness lingered like a heavy fog, and the entities she encountered were both enchanting and terrifying in equal measure. Gigantic creatures with eyes like burning coals, their forms twisting in

The guardian veil

unnatural ways, watching her with hungry intent. Others were less tangible, mere whispers of shadow that flickered in and out of existence, testing her will and courage with every encounter.

Evelyn stepped into the next realm, the **Dimension of Reflections**, and immediately felt a chill crawl up her spine. The air was dense and cold, like a forgotten cavern, and the world around her seemed unnervingly still. Mirrors stretched endlessly in every direction, their silver surfaces shimmering faintly. Each reflection caught fragments of her movements, but the images weren't quite right.

As she moved deeper into the realm, she saw herself in the mirrors—not as she was, but as she had once been. In one, she was the scared little girl who had run from failure. In another, the overwhelmed young woman who had doubted her own worth. Each reflection stared back with piercing eyes, their expressions filled with anger, sadness, or disappointment.

Then the reflections stepped out of the mirrors.

They solidified into shadowy versions of herself, their forms dark and smoky, their voices twisted echoes of her own. They surrounded her, blocking every possible path forward.

"You cannot hide from us," one said, its voice low and biting.

"We are your fears," whispered another, its tone cold and mocking.

"We are your failures," added a third, its dark eyes narrowing. "And you cannot move forward until you face us."

Evelyn's chest tightened as she took a step back, her heart racing. These weren't just shadows—they were pieces of her. The doubts she had buried, the insecurities she had refused to confront, the pain she had ignored.

"You must conquer us to gain the next seed," one taunted, stepping closer.

Chapter 4

For a moment, Evelyn wanted to run. The weight of their words, their accusations, pressed heavily against her chest. But then she stopped and took a deep breath.

"No," she said firmly, her voice steady despite the fear bubbling beneath the surface. "I won't run from you."

The shadows hesitated, their forms flickering.

"You're a part of me," Evelyn continued, standing taller now. "I've made mistakes. I've doubted myself. But that doesn't define who I am. I'm more than my failures, and I won't let my fears control me."

The shadows grew restless, their edges blurring. They lashed out, their voices rising in a chaotic chorus of taunts and jeers. Evelyn clenched her fists, her resolve hardening. Instead of fighting them, she stepped forward, embracing the shadows.

She didn't push them away or try to destroy them. She faced each one, acknowledged its presence, and accepted it for what it was—a part of her past.

As she did, the shadows began to fade, their forms dissolving into wisps of smoke. The mirrors shattered, their jagged fragments glinting briefly before vanishing into the void.

The air shifted, growing lighter, and at the center of the dimension, a shimmering light appeared. It pulsed softly, warm and inviting. Evelyn approached it, her heart steady, and reached out.

The second **Aetheric Seed** hovered before her, glowing with a radiant light that filled the space with hope and renewal. As her fingers closed around it, she felt a surge of energy—calm and empowering—flow through her.

The dimension around her began to fade, the oppressive stillness replaced by a gentle warmth. Evelyn took a deep breath and smiled faintly. She had faced her fears and found strength

The guardian veil

in her vulnerabilities. With the second seed in hand, she was ready to return to the guardians.

Five

Chapter 5

Evelyn stepped into the Chamber of Unity, the second Aetheric Seed nestled safely in her hands. Its gentle glow pulsed faintly, as though it resonated with her heartbeat. The Guardians stood in their usual places, and despite the serenity of the chamber, Evelyn's heart felt heavy, burdened by the knowledge she had gained and the trials still ahead.

She raised her eyes to the Guardian of Time, whose presence exuded both patience and authority. "What if I fail?" she asked, her voice quiet but laced with fear. "What if I can't protect the Veil?"

The Guardian of Time regarded her with an expression that seemed both understanding and unyielding. "The danger lies in overestimating yourself or underestimating the challenge," he said, his voice smooth yet firm. "The Veil is delicate, Evelyn. It must be respected as much as it is understood. Each time

The guardian veil

you cross into another dimension, you leave a trace of yourself behind. And with each crossing, the shadows take notice."

Evelyn's grip on the seed tightened as a chill ran down her spine. "Shadows?" she echoed.

"They are drawn to your light," the Guardian of Light interjected, stepping forward. Her radiant form seemed to dim slightly, as if the mention of the shadows brought with it an inevitable darkness. "These entities thrive on the unraveling of balance. They will seek to exploit your presence, to corrupt and weaken your resolve. You must remain vigilant."

Evelyn felt the weight of their warnings pressing down on her. The enormity of her task loomed larger than ever, yet a spark of determination flared within her. "I won't let them corrupt my home," she vowed, her voice steady despite the fear threatening to creep in. "I'll do whatever it takes to stop them."

The Guardians exchanged glances, their expressions unreadable. It was Liora who stepped forward, her wings shimmering faintly in the chamber's light. "Good," she said, her tone both encouraging and cautious. "But know this—time is of the essence. The more seeds you gather, the stronger your connection to the Veil will become. And the stronger your connection, the more attention you will draw from the shadows."

Liora's gaze softened as she continued. "You must also protect the creation link—the thread that binds the realms together. If that link is severed, the Veil cannot be restored. Every step you take now is critical, Evelyn. The stakes will only grow higher."

Evelyn nodded, her resolve hardening. She didn't fully understand the creation link, but she knew one thing: she couldn't allow it to fall apart. "I'll keep it intact," she promised, sitting cross-legged among the towering forms of the Guardians

Chapter 5

and trying not to fidget under their penetrating gazes. She felt like the awkward kid at a parent-teacher conference, except her "teachers" were cosmic beings, and the stakes were a little higher than a bad report card. Her pulse quickened as Liora moved even closer than before.

"We are not mere watchers," Liora began, her voice calm but powerful. "We are the architects of the Matrix—a sanctuary forged long ago to protect and nurture the evolving human psyche. The Matrix is a realm of experience, growth, and learning, shielding humanity from the overwhelming complexities of the multiverse."

Evelyn raised an eyebrow. "So… it's like training wheels for the universe?"

The Guardian of Wisdom chuckled, the sound like the rustling of ancient scrolls. "A crude comparison, but not entirely inaccurate," he said, his form flickering with cascading symbols.

"But why create such boundaries?" Evelyn asked, her brow furrowed in genuine confusion. "Why limit what we can see, what we can understand?"

"The human mind," Wisdom replied, his voice deep and resonant, "is a delicate construct. To expose it to the chaotic energies of the multiverse too soon would be disastrous. Without the Matrix, humanity would face madness, despair, and the dissolution of all reason. Our duty has always been to nurture—to set these guardrails so your species can develop organically."

Evelyn leaned back slightly, crossing her arms as she considered this. "Okay, I get the whole 'protection from chaos' thing," she said, "but here I am, standing in your fancy cosmic conference room. If the Matrix is so necessary, why am I able to breach it?"

The Guardians exchanged glances, their expressions unreadable. It was the Guardian of Light who spoke next, her form glowing softly like the first rays of dawn. "Your awakening was not intended," she said, her voice carrying both warmth and a hint of caution.

"Not intended?" Evelyn repeated, arching a skeptical eyebrow. "So… what? I'm like a cosmic oops?"

The Guardian of Darkness let out a low chuckle, his shadowy form rippling like smoke. "Not quite," he said, his voice a rumble. "You tapped into energies that had lain dormant within you, Evelyn. In doing so, you weakened the boundaries of the Matrix."

"Wait, so you're saying this is all my fault?" Evelyn asked, gesturing dramatically at the chamber. "Great. First, I can't keep my houseplants alive, and now I've accidentally broken the fabric of reality. Stellar track record I've got going here."

Liora's wings fluttered faintly, her expression softening. "Your actions were not intentional, but they have consequences nonetheless," she said. "In breaching the Matrix, you became a beacon. Entities that thrive on imbalance and chaos are drawn to your light, seeking to exploit your presence."

"Exploitation?" Evelyn echoed, a chill creeping into her voice.

"Yes," the Guardian of Light confirmed, her glow dimming slightly. "These entities would use you as a key to unravel the boundaries that protect your world. If left unchecked, they will bring ruin."

Evelyn's stomach twisted, the weight of their words settling heavily on her shoulders. "So… I'm not just a cosmic oops—I'm a glowing 'open for business' sign for interdimensional troublemakers."

"Precisely," the Guardian of Wisdom said with a small nod. "Though perhaps with less sarcasm."

Chapter 5

Evelyn sighed, pinching the bridge of her nose. "Okay. So, what do we do about it? I'm guessing the answer isn't just 'ignore it and hope for the best.'"

"It is not," Liora said, stepping closer. "Your journey is perilous, Evelyn, but it is also necessary. You have a unique role to play in restoring the balance. And while your awakening may not have been intended, it is now part of a larger design. We will guide you, but the path ahead is yours to walk."

Evelyn straightened, her unease replaced by a flicker of determination. "Fine," she said, her voice steadying. "I'll walk it. But for the record, I'd like to lodge a formal complaint about the onboarding process. A heads-up would've been nice."

"The Matrix is layered," Liora continued, her eyes shimmered with faint light, as though reflecting unseen worlds. "Each layer corresponds to different levels of consciousness and understanding. The physical realm you occupy is merely the outermost layer, designed to shield you from the harsher truths of the multiverse. But beneath it lies a spectrum of existence, intricate and infinite, waiting to be explored."

Evelyn leaned forward slightly, her curiosity piqued despite the overwhelming circumstances. "So… you're saying the reality I've known all my life is just the surface of some cosmic onion?"

Liora's lips curved into a faint smile. "A somewhat colorful metaphor, but not inaccurate."

The Guardian of Space stepped forward, her form rippling like a starry expanse. "Precisely," she said, her voice vast and echoing, as though it came from the farthest corners of the universe. "We Guardians ensure that the fundamental laws of this layered reality remain intact—laws that govern time, emotion, energy, and existence itself. Each seed you gather strengthens these bonds and fortifies the Veil, preserving the balance within the Matrix."

Evelyn rubbed her temples, trying to wrap her head around the concept. "So, basically, I'm reinforcing reality so it doesn't unravel into some kind of cosmic free-for-all?"

"Exactly," the Guardian of Space confirmed, her tone slightly amused.

"That's… comforting," Evelyn muttered, though the enormity of her task was anything but.

As the room grew silent, she pondered the implications of her role. She was now part of something so vast and complex it made her previous worries—unpaid bills, forgotten deadlines—seem laughably small. But the responsibility weighed heavily on her shoulders. She wasn't just a protector; she was also a potential disruptor, walking a thin line between preserving the balance and breaking it entirely.

"If I stop these entities," she began, her voice quieter now, "will we be safe? Will the Matrix be stable again?"

"For a time, yes," the Guardian of Time replied thoughtfully, his golden halo spinning slowly. "But understand this: the Matrix is not a static creation. It is alive, evolving with every choice, every ripple. New threats will always arise. New beings will seek to bend the fabric of existence to their will."

Evelyn exhaled sharply, crossing her arms as she processed his words. "So, basically, even if I pull this off, it's like sweeping up the sand while the tide keeps rolling in."

"An apt comparison," Wisdom said, his tone even. "But every action taken to preserve balance strengthens the foundation, ensuring that the tide does not overwhelm all at once."

"Great," Evelyn muttered under her breath. "I'm a cosmic janitor now. All I need is a mop and a motivational poster."

Chapter 5

The Guardian of Darkness chuckled lowly, his shadowy form rippling. "You may find that humor will serve you well on this journey, Evelyn. It is a spark of light in the shadows, and the entities you face will do everything to snuff it out."

As Evelyn leaned against the crystalline wall, listening intently, the Guardians began to share stories of their past struggles—battles fought in the shadows of existence to preserve the fragile balance of the Matrix. Each tale revealed not just their power but the immense cost of their duty.

"In the early days," the Guardian of Darkness began, his voice a low rumble that echoed through the chamber, "we faced a being known as the Fracture. It was unlike anything we had encountered—neither light nor shadow but a force of pure entropy. It sought to unravel the Matrix, to rewrite existence itself into a form devoid of order or purpose."

Evelyn shuddered, trying to picture something so destructive. "What would that even look like?" she asked, her voice quiet but curious.

"Chaos," the Guardian of Wisdom interjected, his glowing form pulsing faintly. "A reality where nothing is constant. Memories erased before they are formed, emotions flickering like flames in a storm. Humanity would have been consumed by despair and madness, unable to anchor themselves to any truth."

The chamber grew heavy with the weight of the story. Evelyn could almost feel the echoes of that ancient struggle, a tension that lingered even now.

"We fought the Fracture for eons," Darkness continued, his shadowy form shifting as though recalling the battle itself. "It shattered the Matrix, scattering the layers like shards of glass. Humanity faltered, caught in the void, but we reclaimed the

The guardian veil

fragments and reconstructed what was lost. Piece by piece, we rebuilt the Matrix, creating a sanctuary where humanity could heal and grow."

"And yet," Liora added, her voice soft but firm, "the remnants of such beings linger in the shadows, waiting. They watch for moments of weakness, for signs that the Veil is thinning."

Evelyn's pulse quickened, her mind racing. "What happened to the Fracture?" she asked, captivated by the tale.

The Guardians exchanged glances, their expressions grim. It was the Guardian of Light who finally spoke, her radiance dimming slightly. "It was contained but not destroyed," she said. "Beings of such power cannot be unmade, only subdued. The Fracture lies dormant, sealed within the deepest layers of the Matrix, where its influence is diminished. But the seal is not impervious."

"Locked within a dimensional prison," the Guardian of Longevity said, stepping forward. His voice was deep and resonant, carrying the weight of untold millennia. His form was regal, like a tree forged of bronze and amber, with branches extending from his shoulders and leaves that shimmered like molten gold. "But even in its confinement, the Fracture's essence seeps through the edges of your realm, feeding on confusion and fear. It thrives on the cracks created by humanity's unawareness."

Evelyn's stomach churned as the implications sank in. "And that fear…" she said slowly, pieces of the puzzle clicking into place. "It's awakened something within me, hasn't it? Is that why I'm here? To confront the Fracture?"

The Guardians exchanged another glance, their ancient wisdom woven into their silence. Finally, it was Liora who stepped forward, "Potentially, yes," she said, her voice gentle

Chapter 5

but firm. "But your task now is not to face the Fracture directly. First, you must gather the remaining Aetheric Seeds. Only then can we fortify the Veil and protect your world from those who wish to unravel it."

Evelyn exhaled sharply, rubbing her temples. "Right. No big deal," she muttered. "Just collect cosmic puzzle pieces, save the Veil, and maybe, if I'm really lucky, avoid being obliterated by interdimensional chaos."

The Guardian of Longevity's lips twitched, almost forming a smile. "You are not alone, Evelyn. We are here to guide you, but the path ahead will test you in ways you cannot yet imagine. You carry light within you, but light alone will not be enough to win this fight."

"And what exactly will be enough?" Evelyn asked, raising an eyebrow.

"Courage," the Guardian of Darkness intoned, his shadowy form rippling. "And the willingness to accept what you fear most. The Fracture is not merely a force; it is a reflection of the cracks within all beings. To face it, you must first understand yourself."

Evelyn felt the weight of his words settle over her. "So, let me get this straight," she said, crossing her arms. "Not only do I have to run around collecting these seeds while dodging shadow monsters, but I also have to face my deepest fears and confront some existential chaos entity that's leaking into my world? Fantastic. Totally manageable."

Liora's gentle laugh broke the tension, her light glowing a little brighter. "You have more strength than you realize, Evelyn," she said. "And you will not walk this path alone. The seeds will guide you, just as your light guides us. Trust in the journey, even when the way forward seems unclear."

Chapter 6

Days blurred into each other as Evelyn trained under the Guardians' watchful eyes. Each session pushed her to the limits of her endurance—and occasionally, her patience. Navigating unseen dimensions was as disorienting as trying to walk a straight line on a spinning carnival ride.

"Again," Liora instructed one morning, her wings glowing faintly as Evelyn stumbled back from yet another failed attempt to stabilize a rift.

"I swear, these dimensions have it out for me," Evelyn muttered, brushing dirt—or whatever passed for dirt in this realm—off her pants. "I step left, the world tilts right. I step right, and suddenly, gravity's on vacation."

The Guardian of Darkness let out a low chuckle, his smoky form rippling. "Perhaps they sense your frustration," he said. "You must learn to bend with the chaos, not fight it."

Chapter 6

"Bend with the chaos," Evelyn repeated, rolling her eyes. "Great. I'll just add 'cosmic yoga' to my ever-growing skill set."

Despite her grumbling, she was improving. Each day brought new challenges, and with them, small victories. She gathered more seeds, each one a glowing fragment of the Matrix's delicate fabric. They weren't just sources of power—they carried memories and echoes of the past. Some were joyous: laughter from forgotten eras, moments of kindness etched into the threads of existence. Others were heavier, filled with sorrow and loss.

One evening, after a particularly grueling day of exploration, Evelyn sat beneath the soft glow of the chamber's crystalline walls. The latest seed she had retrieved pulsed faintly in her hand, its light warm but somber.

"Why must knowledge bring such weight?" she asked aloud, her voice weary.

The Guardian of Light, who had been silently observing her, stepped forward. Her radiant form dimmed slightly, as if to match Evelyn's mood. "Awareness comes at a cost," she said gently. "The more you learn, the heavier the burden becomes. Gratitude often intertwines with sorrow, for knowledge reveals the fragility of existence. The Matrix thrives on this balance, and so must you."

Evelyn nodded, turning the seed over in her hand. "Great," she muttered. "Existential crises wrapped up in glowing orbs. Just what I needed."

But beneath the sarcasm, she felt the truth of the Guardian's words settle deep within her. The more she understood, the more she realized how delicate the balance truly was—and how easily it could be broken.

"And if I fail?" she asked, her voice softer now, almost hesitant.

The guardian veil

"What becomes of us then?"

Liora stepped closer, her presence a calming contrast to Evelyn's rising unease. "You will not fail," she said firmly. "You were chosen because you possess a unique spark—a reflection of the light within the Matrix itself. As long as you cherish the bonds of your humanity, you will find strength in adversity."

Evelyn let out a shaky breath, a small smile tugging at her lips. "No pressure, right?" she said, tucking the seed into her satchel.

Liora's wings shimmered faintly, a gesture of reassurance. "Pressure shapes diamonds, Evelyn. And you shine brighter than you realize."

Evelyn snorted, standing and brushing herself off. "Let's hope that shine doesn't make me an even bigger target for the shadow monsters."

"Perhaps," Darkness said, his deep voice laced with humor. "But the brighter the light, the deeper the shadows must reach to extinguish it. That is their weakness, Evelyn—and your strength."

###

With the Aetheric Seeds safely secured, Evelyn stood at the threshold of a new challenge. The air around her thrummed with anticipation, the chamber's crystalline walls glowing faintly as if the Matrix itself was watching. The Guardians formed a circle around her, their presence both comforting and formidable.

"Remember," the Guardian of Wisdom said, his shimmering form steady and calm, "you are not only a traveler but a protector. The Matrix thrives on the connections between you and your kind. Those bonds are its lifeblood. Use your understanding to defend and reinforce them."

Evelyn nodded, feeling a swell of determination rise within

Chapter 6

her. Each seed she had gathered had taught her something vital—about herself, about the Matrix, and about the delicate threads that held existence together. She was no longer the unsure archivist who had stumbled into a world she didn't understand. She had grown, shaped by the trials she had faced and the lessons she had learned.

"You've come far," Liora said, stepping forward. Her wings shimmered with a soft, golden light that felt like a warm embrace. "But the greatest challenges lie ahead. The entities that lurk in the shadows have sensed your progress. They will not wait idly. Be prepared for their resistance."

Evelyn tightened the strap of her satchel, where the seeds pulsed faintly, each one a testament to her journey. "I'm ready," she said, her voice steady. "I've come too far to back down now."

"Good," the Guardian of Darkness intoned, his shadowy form rippling like smoke. "Remember, the entities you face will seek to exploit your fears and doubts. But the strength you carry—your light—will always burn brighter than their shadows if you let it."

The path ahead shimmered, a glowing expanse that seemed to stretch into infinity. It was both inviting and foreboding, a perfect reflection of the journey she was about to undertake.

As Evelyn stepped forward, the Guardian of Space spoke, her voice echoing with infinite depth. "The bonds you've reinforced are not just for your world, Evelyn. The Matrix is vast, its threads stretching across countless dimensions. Protecting one protects many. Do not forget this."

Evelyn paused, turning back to look at the Guardians one last time. Their forms stood tall and unwavering, a reminder of the strength she could draw upon. "I won't forget," she said, her voice resolute.

The guardian veil

With that, she stepped through the threshold, the light enveloping her in a warm, radiant embrace.

—-

The realm she entered was unlike anything she had seen before. The air shimmered with a strange, iridescent quality, and the ground beneath her feet felt both solid and fluid. Shapes twisted and turned in the distance, their forms impossible to define. Evelyn's heart raced, but she forced herself to breathe deeply.

She wasn't alone. The seeds in her satchel pulsed faintly, their light cutting through the strange haze. They were a reminder of her purpose—a beacon in the unknown.

As she ventured further, the air grew colder, and the shadows seemed to stretch longer. A faint whisper reached her ears, soft at first but growing louder with each step. It wasn't words exactly, but an unsettling hum that made the hairs on her neck stand on end.

"Alright," Evelyn muttered to herself, gripping the strap of her satchel tighter. "Let's see what you've got."

The whispers grew into a low growl as the first shadow emerged, its form twisting unnaturally, eyes glowing with a malevolent light. Evelyn's breath hitched, but she stood her ground, her determination burning brighter than her fear.

This was her fight. And she wasn't backing down.

Seven

Chapter 7

Evelyn stumbled out of the radiant portal and landed unceremoniously in what we'll call the backyard. Dirt sprayed across her sneakers as she groaned, brushing glowing particles from her hair. She straightened her satchel and glared at the shimmering remnants of the portal as it disappeared.

"Easy, they said," she muttered, mimicking the ethereal voices of the Guardians. "Transform your world, they said. It'll be rewarding. Yeah, right."

The seeds pulsed faintly in her satchel, as if to mock her. She flung it on the porch and sank onto the nearest garden chair, crossing her arms. "You don't get it," she said to no one in particular. "First, I had to wrestle a shadow beast with more teeth than a dentist's worst nightmare. Then I faced that 'trial of fears' thing, which—spoiler alert—turned out to be me accidentally walking into a room full of my middle school yearbook photos. And *now*? Now I have to 'speak the language of humanity's fears and hopes'? Have they *met* people? We barely agree on pizza toppings!"

As if in response, The wind almost breezed through her. She then sighed and pulled the satchel closer. The seeds, despite her irritation, gave off a calming warmth. She rolled her eyes at them. "Oh, now you're sweet. Where was this energy when I was being chased by that weird dimension worm?"

She thought back to her final task in the strange iridescent realm. It had gone suspiciously well—too well, actually. Evelyn squinted at the sky, suspicion creeping into her mind. The Guardian of Space had said something about "trials scaling to your potential." Had they… underestimated her? She snorted.

"Figures," she muttered. "They probably took one look at me and thought, 'Oh, she can't handle the big scary trials. Let's make it easy.' Joke's on them—I'm tougher than I look."

Still, there had been some moments of hilarity. Like when the shadow beast got its claws tangled in its own tail mid-attack, or when the Trial of Resilience turned into a game of dodgeball against sentient vines that kept tripping over each other.

Evelyn found herself laughing despite her annoyance. "Honestly, they could've just sent me to babysit a group of toddlers for an hour if they wanted to test my patience. That's way scarier."

As the glow of the seeds pulsed stronger, she sighed again and stood up. "Alright, alright, I'll plant you. But I swear, if one of you sprouts a tree that insults me every morning, I'm sending you back to the Guardians with a strongly worded complaint."

She grabbed a trowel and headed to the garden. The earth felt soft under her hands, and as she placed the seeds into the soil, a strange sense of peace washed over her. For all her grumbling,

Chapter 7

she knew the Guardians were right. Humanity needed these seeds.

The first seed emitted a soft hum as she covered it with dirt. A tiny sprout emerged instantly, shimmering faintly. Evelyn couldn't help but smile. "Okay, that's actually pretty cool."

Her smile turned sly. "But if anyone asks, I'm telling them this was *super* hard. Heroic-level stuff. No one's gonna take me seriously if I admit it was easier than beating my brother at Mario Kart."

As she worked, Evelyn felt a renewed sense of purpose. The Guardians' words echoed in her mind, and for the first time, she believed she could help her world heal. Even if it meant dealing with skepticism, fear, and, occasionally, the complete absurdity of human nature.

She stood back and surveyed her work, hands on her hips. "Well, seeds," she said, smirking. "Let's see if you can handle *my* world. It's a lot messier than the Matrix, trust me."

The seeds glowed brightly, as if accepting her challenge.

###

Evelyn emerged in her small apartment in Eldoria, the late afternoon sun warming her skin as she stepped through the door. Before she could even set her satchel down, a gray blur darted across the room, and Nimbus launched himself at her feet.

"Whoa, buddy!" Evelyn exclaimed, stumbling slightly as the fluffy missile wrapped himself around her ankles, purring like a motorboat. "Miss me?"

Nimbus meowed in response, his golden eyes narrowing as if to say, *You have no idea how boring it's been without you.*

She scooped him up, his fur soft and warm against her face. "Well, someone's needy," she said, scratching behind his ears.

The guardian veil

Nimbus let out a chirping trill, half complaint and half affection, before squirming in her arms. She set him down, and he immediately began weaving between her legs, tail held high like a flag of triumph.

"I hope you didn't destroy anything while I was gone," she said, narrowing her eyes at him. Nimbus responded by leaping onto the windowsill, where a suspiciously toppled stack of books sat precariously close to the edge.

Evelyn sighed, brushing glowing particles off her jacket and tossing her satchel onto the couch. "You're lucky I'm too tired to scold you properly." Nimbus meowed again, clearly unbothered, and began pawing at the strap of her bag.

"Not a toy, Nim," she warned, pulling the satchel away. But as she did, the faint hum of the seeds inside seemed to catch his attention. Nimbus froze, his ears twitching.

"What?" Evelyn asked, tilting her head. Nimbus stared at the bag with laser focus, then gave a tentative paw tap to its side.

"You're weird," she muttered, ruffling his fur as she walked toward the kitchen. "But I'll feed you first before I go saving the world again."

—-

After a quick snack for Nimbus (and a piece of toast for herself), Evelyn grabbed her satchel and headed for the door. Nimbus trailed behind her like a shadow, his tail flicking with curiosity.

"You're staying here," she said, pointing a finger at him. Nimbus responded by sitting down and licking his paw, clearly unconcerned by her decree.

"Don't look at me like that," Evelyn said, pulling the door shut behind her. "This is a one-person mission."

The city buzzed all around her, alive with its usual chaos—

Chapter 7

honking cars, chattering crowds, and the occasional street performer playing way too loudly. But to Evelyn, everything looked... different. Like someone had turned up the contrast on reality. The buildings seemed taller, the air felt heavier, and the sunlight hitting the pavement practically sparkled.

She wandered through the streets, her satchel swinging at her side. People rushed past, their faces set in frowns or totally zoned out, probably thinking about deadlines, dinner, or whatever stress of the day was bugging them. Evelyn paused at a crosswalk and watched a delivery guy nearly wipe out on his bike, a mom juggling a stroller and grocery bags, and a guy yelling into his phone like it owed him money.

"They don't see it," she muttered, shaking her head. "No one notices how connected everything is. How freaking *amazing* it all is."

She adjusted her satchel and kept walking. After everything she'd been through—the wild realms, the crazy trials, and the terrifying shadow monsters—she couldn't unsee it. The threads that held the world together were all around her, but no one seemed to notice.

Well, if no one else was going to wake up to it, she figured she'd have to start somewhere.

Her feet carried her to the library, the place where everything had started. The massive stone building loomed ahead like some kind of ancient fortress, the worn steps leading up to heavy wooden doors that creaked like a haunted house. Evelyn smiled to herself. She'd always liked the library's vibe—quiet, a little mysterious, and full of stories.

Inside, the usual smell of old books and lemon-scented cleaner hit her. Students sat at tables surrounded by stacks of notes, librarians whispered like they were sharing government secrets, and someone nearby sneezed loud enough to shake the shelves.

She headed to the back, to a corner of the archives where it was always cool and quiet. Kneeling by a planter filled with fresh soil, she reached into her satchel and pulled out one of the seeds. It glowed softly in her hand, warm and steady, almost like it was alive.

"Okay," she whispered to herself. "Here goes nothing."

She pressed the seed into the soil and sat back, holding her breath. For a second, nothing happened. Then the dirt shifted, and a tiny sprout poked through, its leaves sparkling like they were covered in glitter. It gave off this soft, calming hum that she could feel in her chest.

Evelyn grinned. "Alright, that's pretty cool."

Evelyn stayed kneeling by the planter, staring at the tiny, glowing sprout. It was beautiful, almost mesmerizing, but it was more than that—it *meant* something. It was proof of everything she'd seen, everything she'd experienced in the multiverse. This little plant was a beginning, a spark of hope rooted right here in her world.

She reached out, her fingers brushing the delicate leaves, and the faint hum seemed to grow warmer, deeper, as if the sprout was trying to tell her something. The hum wasn't just sound—it was a feeling. A connection.

"That's it," Evelyn murmured, sitting back on her heels. The idea was forming in her mind now, a flicker that quickly grew into a flame. "If people could *see* this—feel this—they'd understand. They'd know there's more to the world than what's right in front of them."

She glanced around the quiet archive room, her heart racing.

Chapter 7

The thought of sharing this, of trying to explain everything she'd learned, was as thrilling as it was terrifying. After all, she could barely wrap her own head around it most days. How could she get other people to believe her?

Her gaze fell to the sprout again, its glow steady and calming. "Start small," she said softly. "Plant the seed, see what grows."

###

By the time Evelyn left the library that evening, her mind was buzzing with plans.

Organizing the gathering hadn't been easy. In fact, it was probably harder than some of the trials Evelyn had faced in the multiverse. At least shadow beasts didn't require a permit for snacks.

The idea had come to her late one night as she scribbled in her journal, Nimbus snoozing beside her. If the Guardians wanted her to plant seeds of knowledge, she figured she could start literally *and* figuratively. A community event seemed like the perfect way to share her story—or at least as much as people could handle without thinking she'd lost her mind.

The next day, she nervously approached Mrs. Eddington, the head librarian, who was known for her no-nonsense attitude and love of neatly organized paperwork. Evelyn half-expected her to shoot the idea down on the spot.

"You want to hold a... multiverse awareness event?" Mrs. Eddington had asked, peering over her glasses with a mix of curiosity and suspicion.

"Well, kind of," Evelyn replied, fiddling with the strap of her satchel. "It's more about... connections. You know, helping people see the bigger picture and appreciate the world around them."

To her surprise, Mrs. Eddington nodded. "Sounds unusual,

but interesting. We'll schedule it for Friday evening. I assume you'll handle the setup?"

Evelyn left the library that day with a mix of excitement and dread. The next few days were full of planning. She designed a simple flyer—*"Awareness of the Multiverse: A Conversation About Connection and Awareness"*—and posted it around the neighborhood. She bought snacks (mostly because she figured free food would at least get people in the door) and spent hours in the archives, rehearsing what she'd say. Nimbus, ever the helpful companion, spent most of that time either sitting on her notes or batting pens off the table.

The turnout wasn't massive, but it wasn't terrible either. About a dozen people showed up, ranging from curious teens to retirees looking for something to do on a Friday night. Evelyn had set up the reading room with folding chairs and a small table for refreshments. She even added a vase of flowers to make the space feel less intimidating—though Nimbus promptly knocked it over right before the event started.

As she stepped up to the podium that evening, Evelyn's stomach churned with nerves. What if no one took her seriously? What if they thought she was completely nuts?

But then she looked out at the small group of faces, some curious, some skeptical, and felt a spark of determination. She wasn't here to convince anyone. She was here to share what she'd learned and let the seeds take root on their own.

Her palms were sweaty, and her notes trembled slightly in her hands, but as she opened her mouth to speak, the words flowed naturally.

Evelyn took a steadying breath, her gaze sweeping over the small group gathered in the library's reading room. Their eyes

Chapter 7

were fixed on her, some wide with curiosity, others narrowed with skepticism. A few were polite but clearly guarded, like they'd been dragged along by a friend and weren't sure what they'd signed up for.

She clutched the edges of the podium, her notes trembling slightly in her hands. "Thank you all for coming," she began, her voice steady but edged with nervous energy. "I know your time is valuable, and I'm grateful you're spending some of it here."

A faint murmur of acknowledgment rippled through the room. Evelyn smiled, just barely.

"What if I told you," she said, leaning forward slightly, "that this world—our physical realm—is just one layer of something much bigger? That we're all part of a vast, interconnected tapestry of existence?"

The silence in the room was deafening. Evelyn could feel the weight of their attention pressing on her, but it wasn't entirely uncomfortable. It was... expectant.

"I know it sounds strange," she continued, her voice gaining confidence. "But I've seen it. I've walked through places where reality bends and shifts in ways we can't imagine. I've met beings who protect the balance of these realms—Guardians who entrusted me with a mission to safeguard our world."

She paused, letting the words sink in.

A woman in the front row, sharp glasses perched on her nose, raised her hand. "Are you saying there's a *multiverse*?" she asked, her tone half-challenging, half-intrigued. "That we're not alone?"

"Yes!" Evelyn exclaimed, the word tumbling out with more enthusiasm than she'd intended. "Exactly. The multiverse isn't just theory—it's real. And it's incredible. It's full of light and

The guardian veil

beauty, but also shadow and danger. Everything is connected, and that connection is fragile. That's why we need to respect the boundaries that protect us."

A man in the back—the one Evelyn had mentally dubbed *Snack Guy*—piped up. "So, like... this is some kind of superhero thing? Are we gonna get powers or what?"

Evelyn laughed, the tension in the room breaking slightly. "No capes, I promise," she said with a grin. "But it's not about powers. It's about awareness. The Guardians taught me that understanding the connections between us—between everything—makes us stronger. Ignorance creates fear, and fear can break those connections. But awareness? That's how we overcome our limitations."

The room buzzed with murmurs as her words settled over the group. Some people nodded, their faces thoughtful. Others frowned, their skepticism still firmly in place. Evelyn didn't mind. She wasn't here to convince them outright. She was here to plant an idea and let it grow.

"I know this all sounds crazy," she admitted, raising her hands. "But just think about it. What if the world is more connected than we've ever realized? What if the little things we do—how we treat each other, how we see the world—actually matter more than we think?"

The woman in the front row folded her arms but gave Evelyn a slight nod. "It's a lot to take in," she said.

"It is," Evelyn agreed, her voice softening. "But big changes always start small. Even just being here tonight, asking these questions—that's a start."

Despite her passionate presentation, not everyone was on board. As the library event wound down, Evelyn overheard snippets of conversation that stung more than she wanted to

Chapter 7

admit.

"She's probably just read too much science fiction," one person muttered on their way out.

"Yeah, sounds like someone with an overactive imagination," another agreed, shaking their head.

Evelyn smiled politely as they left, but the doubt they planted lingered. Was she asking too much of people? Expecting them to believe her wild stories about Guardians, glowing seeds, and a fragile multiverse?

Back in her apartment that night, Evelyn slumped into her chair, Nimbus hopping onto her lap with an empathetic meow. She absently scratched his head, staring at the notebook she'd used to plan her presentation.

"Maybe they're right, Nim," she murmured. "Maybe this is too much for people to take in."

Nimbus batted at the pen on the desk, sending it rolling to the floor. Evelyn sighed but couldn't help a small smile. "You're right," she said, picking it up. "Giving up isn't going to help. If they can't see the big picture yet, maybe I need to try something smaller."

The next morning, Evelyn started brainstorming again. Instead of just *telling* people about the multiverse, she needed to help them *feel* it—to experience those connections for themselves.

Her first idea was a series of workshops. She rented a small room at a community center and spread the word through flyers and social media posts. "Explore the Hidden Dimensions of Creativity," the flyers read. It wasn't quite "Save the Veil," but it was a start.

The workshops were simple but carefully designed. Evelyn blended storytelling with hands-on activities like painting and

The guardian veil

journaling. She guided meditations, encouraging participants to listen to their intuition and notice the threads of connection in their own lives.

At first, turnout was sparse, and Evelyn faced more skepticism. People struggled to connect with the exercises, brushing them off as quirky or irrelevant. But Evelyn didn't give up. With every session, she adapted, finding new ways to spark curiosity.

And then, little by little, something shifted.

One day, during a group journaling exercise, a woman hesitantly raised her hand. "I don't know if this means anything," she said, "but I've been having these dreams. They're… different. Like I'm in a place I've never seen, but it feels familiar, too."

Evelyn's heart raced. "That's amazing," she said gently. "Dreams can sometimes carry echoes of things we can't quite explain. What do you feel when you're there?"

The woman smiled shyly. "It feels… peaceful. Like I belong there."

Others began chiming in, sharing their own dreams, strange coincidences, or moments of intuition they couldn't ignore. It wasn't long before the workshop transformed into a space where people felt safe to explore ideas they'd never considered before

Over the weeks, Evelyn watched the group grow—not just in size, but in enthusiasm. They started bringing their own stories and ideas, painting vivid pictures of places they'd only imagined, writing poetry that felt like it came from somewhere beyond their own minds.

One participant, a teenager named Mia, shared a charcoal drawing of a vast, glowing tree. "I don't know why," Mia said, blushing as she held up the sketch. "But I've been dreaming about this. It feels important."

Chapter 7

Evelyn stared at the drawing, her breath catching in her throat. The tree looked eerily similar to one she'd seen in the Realm of Connections, its glowing branches stretching infinitely in every direction.

"You're tapping into something big, Mia," Evelyn said, smiling.

Mia beamed, and the room buzzed with excitement.

Eight

Chapter 8

Months passed, and Evelyn's workshops transformed into something bigger than she could have ever imagined. What started as a handful of curious participants grew into a vibrant community. People brought their art, their stories, and their questions. They shared dreams that felt too vivid to be random, coincidences that seemed too precise to be accidents, and feelings they couldn't quite put into words.

But not everything was as bright as the glowing seeds she had planted. Evelyn began to sense it—a creeping darkness that lingered at the edges of her gatherings. It was subtle at first: a shadowy unease that left some participants questioning their experiences. Then came the whispers. People would tell her about dreams turning into nightmares, feelings of dread clouding the clarity they'd found, and a growing fear of the unknown.

Chapter 8

Evelyn knew what it was. The entities. The same ones that had hunted her in the multiverse were now finding their way into her world, feeding off the growing awareness and using it against them.

Evelyn sat at her desk one evening, Nimbus curled up on a pile of notes like the world's laziest guardian. The light from her desk lamp cast long shadows across the room as she stared at the flyer she'd been designing:

Awakened Connections: A Celebration of Knowledge and Unity

It was meant to be her biggest event yet—a chance to bring everyone together, to show them the beauty of their shared experiences and help them stand strong against the whispers of doubt. But it wasn't just for them. Evelyn knew the event would act as a beacon, drawing the shadows closer. The entities wouldn't let her build this community without a fight.

"Do you think I'm crazy, Nim?" she asked, scratching the cat's ears. Nimbus opened one eye, blinked slowly, and stretched out like he had all the confidence in the world.

"Right," Evelyn muttered. "No pressure."

The evening of the event arrived, and the library's reading room was packed. Folding chairs filled every corner, and a quiet buzz of anticipation filled the air. Evelyn stood at the front, her satchel resting on the floor by her feet, the seeds inside pulsing faintly.

She took a deep breath and stepped forward. "Thank you all for being here," she began, her voice steady but laced with emotion. "This isn't just an event. It's a space to connect, to share, and to grow. The world is bigger than we've ever been taught to believe. Tonight, we're here to celebrate that—and each other."

The guardian veil

The crowd clapped lightly, their expressions a mix of excitement and nervousness. Evelyn continued, drawing on the Guardians' teachings to guide her words. She talked about the power of connection, how awareness could bring both fear and strength, and how facing their doubts together could create something unbreakable.

One by one, people stood to share their stories.

"I've been dreaming about this bridge," a man said. "It stretches into the sky and leads... somewhere. I don't know where, but it feels like I'm supposed to find it."

"I've been seeing colors," another woman added. "When I close my eyes, it's like they're alive, moving and blending. It's beautiful but overwhelming."

Mia, the teenager who'd shared her drawing of the glowing tree weeks ago, stood up next. "The tree," she said, her voice trembling slightly. "I've been dreaming about it again. Only now, there are shadows at the base. They're... watching."

Evelyn's stomach twisted. She could feel it too. The room, once warm and buzzing with energy, had grown colder. The shadows were here.

A chill swept through the room, so faint at first that only Evelyn seemed to notice. But as more people shared their fears and doubts, the whispers began. Quiet, insidious murmurs that crawled along the edges of the gathering.

"What if this isn't real?"

"You're wasting your time."

"This is dangerous. You should leave."

Evelyn gripped the edges of the podium, her pulse racing. She couldn't see the shadows, but she could feel them, coiling like smoke around the room.

She stepped forward, raising her voice. "Listen to me," she

Chapter 8

said, her tone firm but calm. "The fear you're feeling—it's not yours. It's coming from the shadows, from the entities that don't want us to grow. They thrive on doubt, but we're stronger than they are. Together, we can stand against them."

The room was tense, the whispers growing louder, but Evelyn didn't stop. She reached into her satchel and pulled out one of the glowing seeds. Holding it high, she let its light fill the room. The shadows recoiled, their whispers fading into nothing.

"Let's share our fears," Evelyn said, turning to the crowd. "Together. Say them out loud, and let them lose their power."

One by one, people began to speak.

"I'm scared of failing."

"I'm afraid I'll never understand this."

"I don't know if I belong here."

As they spoke, the room grew lighter. The shadows, unable to hold their grip, melted away. The glowing seed in Evelyn's hand pulsed warmly, its hum resonating with the voices of the crowd.

When the last person finished, the room fell silent again. But this time, it wasn't the silence of fear. It was peace.

Evelyn smiled, her heart full. "You see?" she said softly. "Our fears don't define us. They're just shadows. And shadows can't stand against the light we create together."

The crowd erupted into applause, and Evelyn felt tears prick her eyes. The shadows might still linger at the edges, but tonight, they hadn't won. Tonight, the seeds of connection had taken root—and they were growing.

Suddenly the air in the library grew heavy, almost suffocating, as a dark figure began to materialize near the back of the room. It twisted the air around it, the shadows swirling like an

The guardian veil

angry storm. The warm glow of the seed Evelyn had held only moments before now seemed faint in comparison, struggling to hold back the creeping darkness.

Gasps rippled through the crowd. People instinctively moved closer together, their fear was evident, Evelyn's heart raced, but she forced herself to stay rooted to the spot.

The figure solidified, tall and ominous, its form flickering between something vaguely human and something entirely alien. Its voice boomed through the room, shaking the very walls.

"Foolish mortals!" it bellowed, its tone dripping with disdain. "You cannot grasp what lies beyond the Veil. Your minds are fragile; ignorance is your only protection!"

Evelyn took a step forward, her pulse pounding in her ears. Every instinct screamed at her to run, but she refused. Her community was watching her, their faces filled with both fear and hope. This was her moment to stand firm.

"No," she said, her voice trembling but determined. "Ignorance isn't protection—it's a cage. Together, our awareness is our shield against the darkness! We choose understanding over fear!"

The entity laughed, a deep, bone-chilling sound that made the hair on the back of her neck stand up. "Your light is weak," it sneered. "It will falter. And when it does, I will consume every last one of you."

Evelyn swallowed hard, glancing at the people around her. Their faces were a mix of terror and determination. She wasn't alone in this. Not anymore.

She reached into her satchel, her fingers brushing against the seeds she had collected. They pulsed faintly, warm and steady, a reminder of everything she'd learned and the strength she

Chapter 8

carried.

She turned back to the figure, her hands trembling but steady as she pulled one of the seeds out and held it high. "We are stronger together," she declared, her voice rising with each word. "By the bonds we share and the truths we embrace, we fortify the Veil!"

Light burst from the seed, brighter than before, casting the room in a warm, golden glow. The dark figure recoiled, its form writhing as the light reached it.

The crowd, inspired by Evelyn's defiance, began to move closer, forming a circle around the entity. Someone reached out to her, their hand glowing faintly as they joined the light. Then another, and another.

"Together!" Evelyn shouted, her voice steady now. "We push back the darkness!"

The crowd raised their hands, their light joining hers in a dazzling display. The energy in the room shifted, the fear dissolving into something stronger: unity.

The dark figure screamed, its voice echoing as the collective light pressed against it. The shadows it commanded began to flicker and fade, retreating like smoke in the wind.

The air vibrated with power as the circle of light grew stronger, pushing the entity further back. Evelyn felt the warmth of the community's energy surge through her, a powerful current of hope and courage.

With one final burst of light, the entity let out a furious roar and dissolved, leaving only a faint shadow in its wake. The room fell silent, the air still and calm once more.

Evelyn let out a shaky breath, lowering her hands. She turned to face the crowd, their faces glowing with relief and awe.

"We did it," someone whispered.

The guardian veil

"No," Evelyn said, smiling. "*We* did it. Together."

The group broke into cheers, their voices echoing through the library.

As the cheers quieted and the crowd began to gather their things, Evelyn stayed rooted in place, her hands still faintly tingling with the energy they had all created together. The dark figure might have been defeated, but she knew this was far from the end. The battle against ignorance and fear wasn't something that could be won in a single night. It was ongoing, a choice they'd have to make every day.

As the cheers quieted and the crowd began to gather their things, Evelyn stayed rooted in place, her hands still faintly tingling with the energy they had all created together. The dark figure might have been defeated, but she knew this was far from the end. The battle against ignorance and fear wasn't something that could be won in a single night. It was ongoing, a choice they'd have to make every day.

The first rays of dawn crept through the library windows, painting the room in soft golds and pinks. Evelyn looked around at her community and she stepped forward, her voice clear and steady despite the exhaustion tugging at her. "This is just the beginning," she said, her eyes meeting those of the people who had stood with her. "We possess the power to protect our realm by staying aware and connected. Each of us can be a Guardian of our own reality. It's not about fighting shadows or defeating entities—it's about choosing light every day, even when it's hard."

The room fell silent, her words sinking in. One by one, people nodded, their expressions filled with determination.

"What do we do now?" someone asked.

Evelyn smiled. "We create. We explore. We stay curious

Chapter 8

and open. We share what we've learned with others. The seeds we've planted here tonight—both in this room and in ourselves—need to be nourished. That's how we grow. That's how we keep the Veil strong."

The group began to talk among themselves, their voices filled with a new sense of purpose. Ideas flowed freely—workshops to share their experiences, art projects to express their dreams, community events to invite more people into their growing circle.

Mia, the teenager who had drawn the glowing tree, approached Evelyn with her sketchbook clutched tightly to her chest. "Do you think... I could draw more? Maybe even try to, like, paint the things I see in my dreams?"

Evelyn's smile widened. "I think that's exactly what you should do. Your art has the power to help others see what you see, to understand what words can't always explain."

Mia grinned, her excitement lighting up her face, and hurried back to join a group discussing plans for their next gathering.

Nine

Chapter 9

Evelyn's life shifted gears after that fateful night in the library. She now had loads of activity, writing articles with snappy titles like *"The Multiverse Is Closer Than You Think"* and *"How to Spot Connections in Your Everyday Life Without Looking Like a Weirdo."* She hosted workshops on everything from dream journaling to "practical intuition" (which basically involved teaching people how to trust their gut without freaking out about it).

Word spread fast. Local artists began collaborating with her, turning multiverse-inspired visions into murals that brightened up Eldoria's streets. Scientists, intrigued by her workshops, started digging into studies on quantum entanglement and consciousness, hoping to find parallels between Evelyn's tales and their research. Journalists wrote articles trying to make sense of it all, often with headlines like *"Librarian Turned Interdimensional Guru Says We're All Connected—And People Are*

Chapter 9

Listening."

And they were listening.

One evening, as the city's skyline shimmered under the setting sun, Evelyn stood at the library window, gazing out at the world she'd helped shape. Nimbus sat on the sill beside her, tail flicking lazily.

"It's weird," she said aloud, mostly to herself. "I used to think the Matrix was like a cage, something holding us back. But now... it feels like home. Like this huge, endless canvas, and we're finally starting to paint on it."

Nimbus gave her a slow blink, which she interpreted as agreement. Or hunger.

She felt the warmth of the Guardians' presence then, subtle but steady, like a comforting hand on her shoulder. They were always there, a quiet reminder that her journey wasn't just about protecting the Veil or spreading awareness. It was about *belonging*—to the Matrix, to the world, and to the people she'd inspired along the way.

As the weeks turned into months, Evelyn marveled at how much her world had changed. What had started as a small, hesitant community gathering had blossomed into a citywide movement. Discussions about the multiverse weren't just confined to her workshops anymore; they were happening in cafes, parks, classrooms, and even local news broadcasts.

The Guardians' teachings, once dismissed as fantasy, were weaving their way into Eldoria's culture. People weren't just hearing Evelyn's words—they were living them.

—-

In the wake of their encounter with the shadow entity, something in the air had shifted. There was a sense of urgency, yes, but also curiosity—a hunger for more.

The guardian veil

Local scientists, who had once rolled their eyes at the idea of multiple dimensions, began organizing study groups, pulling apart theories of quantum entanglement and energy fields. Artists created works that felt almost alive, their pieces resonating with something deeply spiritual yet undeniably grounded in science. Teachers brought ideas about connection and intuition into their classrooms, challenging their students to think beyond the physical world.

Evelyn found herself constantly moving, balancing her role as a librarian, a mentor, and a reluctant leader of a growing movement. Her workshops expanded, with people spilling out of the library's reading room and into the hallways. She often found herself coordinating smaller groups, each led by one of her trusted participants.

At one particularly lively gathering, Evelyn stood in front of a packed room. The walls were lined with murals created by local artists—swirling depictions of glowing trees, shimmering bridges, and ethereal beings that seemed to pulse with life.

"The story of Adam and Eve," Evelyn began, her voice clear and steady, "has been a part of our understanding for generations. It tells us where we come from, but it doesn't tell us where we're going. It doesn't capture the vastness of our potential."

A murmur rippled through the crowd.

"Our narratives need to evolve," she continued, her gaze sweeping across the room. "Not just to reflect who we are, but to include the truth of what we've learned—about our creators, the Guardians, and the multiverse they've entrusted us to protect."

Someone in the back raised their hand. "So, you're saying we rewrite history?"

Chapter 9

Evelyn smiled. "Not rewrite—expand. The story of Adam and Eve isn't wrong; it's just incomplete. Think of it as the first chapter in a much larger book. And now, we're starting to write the next one."

The room buzzed with excitement, people turning to each other to share their thoughts.

The community didn't just talk—they acted. Books began circulating through Eldoria, filled with the wisdom of the Guardians and the stories of those who had started exploring their dimensions. Mia's artwork graced the covers of many of them, her glowing trees and swirling skies becoming a symbol of the movement.

Workshops popped up everywhere, led by people who had taken Evelyn's teachings to heart. Some focused on lucid dreaming, others on meditation or creative expression. There was even a group dedicated to "quantum gardening," where participants claimed their plants grew better when they meditated near them.

Evelyn couldn't help but laugh when she visited one of their sessions. "If this works," she said, holding up a particularly vibrant tomato, "I'm adding 'gardening guru' to my resume."

Despite the progress, Evelyn knew there were challenges ahead. Not everyone was eager to embrace change. Some groups clung tightly to old beliefs, dismissing the movement as a fad or a threat to tradition.

She addressed these concerns during one of her gatherings. "This isn't about replacing what you believe," she explained. "It's about expanding it. The Guardians don't demand worship or obedience. They want us to understand, to grow, and to protect what connects us."

Her words resonated with many, but there were still those

The guardian veil

who resisted. Evelyn tried not to let it discourage her. After all, change took time, and she had learned to be patient.

Ten

Chapter 10

As the movement grew stronger, Eldoria found itself at a crossroads. What had started as small, curious conversations about the multiverse and the Guardians was now reshaping the way people thought about everything—about themselves, their origins, and their place in the world.

The shift didn't come without friction. Traditional teachings, ones that had been the foundation of society for generations, were now under intense scrutiny. People began asking questions they'd been afraid to ask before.

"Why are we bound to tales of shame and punishment?" a passionate young woman demanded during a packed panel discussion. She stood in the center of the room, her voice clear and defiant. "Why are we told we're broken, sinful, and unworthy? We're here to thrive, not to shrink ourselves between the lines of ancient text—a text that offered us half-truths at best!"

The guardian veil

The crowd erupted in murmurs. Some nodded in agreement, while others looked uncomfortable. Evelyn, sitting at the edge of the panel, leaned forward. She had felt this energy building for months now—a fierce, collective yearning for something more.

"It's not about rejecting the past," Evelyn said gently, her voice cutting through the noise. "It's about recognizing that those stories were just the beginning. They were written to help people understand their world at the time. But we've grown since then. We know more now. And it's okay to ask for more. To want a narrative that empowers us, not one that keeps us afraid."

The young woman nodded, her fiery expression softening slightly. "So, what does that look like?" she asked. "What's the next story?"

Evelyn smiled. "It starts with co-creation."

That word—co-creation—spread like wildfire through the community. For centuries, humanity had been taught that they were the product of divine will, shaped and molded by forces beyond their understanding. Now, people began to see themselves not as passive participants, but as partners in the act of creation.

The idea of co-creation ignited a fire of curiosity within the community, sparking collaborations that had once seemed impossible. Thinkers, artists, scientists, and spiritual leaders came together, united by a shared desire to learn more—not just about themselves but about the Guardians and the multiverse they were all part of.

"We've learned so much already," Evelyn said during one of their gatherings, standing at the center of a room buzzing with ideas. "But there's still so much we don't know. What if we

Chapter 10

asked the Guardians directly? What if we invited them here?"

The room fell silent as everyone absorbed her words.

"You mean... talk to them?" a young artist asked, her eyes wide.

"Why not?" Evelyn replied. "They've guided us this far. If we reach out with intention, with respect, I think they'll listen."

###

The day of the invitation arrived, and the entire city buzzed with nervous anticipation. The central square of Eldoria, usually filled with the sounds of street vendors and musicians, had been transformed into a space brimming with energy and intent. Murals depicting swirling galaxies and luminous Guardians adorned every wall, and strings of glowing lights crisscrossed overhead, casting a warm glow over the gathering crowd.

Evelyn stood at the forefront, her palms slightly sweaty as she clutched her satchel. Nimbus perched on a nearby table, his tail flicking in annoyance at the growing noise.

"Don't give me that look," she muttered to him. "You're not the one about to summon interdimensional beings in front of half the city."

Nimbus blinked lazily, as if to say, *Your problem, not mine.*

Evelyn took a deep breath and turned to face the crowd. People of all ages had gathered—scientists clutching notebooks, artists holding sketchpads, and curious onlookers who had no idea what to expect. The air was thick with excitement, hope, and just a hint of fear.

"All right," Evelyn called out, her voice steady despite the butterflies in her stomach. "This is it. We've come together today to do something extraordinary. The Guardians have guided us in so many ways, but now it's time to take the next step.

The guardian veil

It's time to reach out and invite them here—to learn directly from them."

The crowd murmured in agreement, their collective energy building.

—-

The ceremony began with a moment of silence, the group focusing their intention on the invitation they wanted to send. Evelyn closed her eyes, the words she'd practiced so many times now rising to the surface.

Guardians, we seek understanding. We seek connection. Help us evolve and explore the mysteries of our existence. Show us the way.

The crowd joined in, their voices intertwining in a steady rhythm. The words carried a weight that seemed to vibrate through the very air.

Then, just as Evelyn was beginning to wonder if it would work, the air shimmered. A cascade of light descended into the square, sparkling and twisting like a living aurora. Gasps rippled through the crowd as the Guardians began to appear, their forms fluid and radiant, each one glowing with an otherworldly light.

Liora stepped forward first, her wings spread wide, their silvery glow contrasting beautifully against the deepening twilight sky. She smiled, her voice resonating with both warmth and power.

"Your audacity to seek truth beyond the confines of fear has drawn us once more," she said, her eyes scanning the gathered crowd.

A young boy near the front tugged on his mother's sleeve. "Audacity means they're impressed, right?" he whispered loudly.

Evelyn stifled a laugh, covering her mouth with her hand.

Chapter 10

Liora, unbothered, inclined her head slightly. "Indeed," she replied, a hint of amusement in her tone.

The Guardian of Wisdom moved forward next, his form resembling a constellation brought to life. "You have taken great strides," he said, his voice deep and measured. "But with understanding comes responsibility. The multiverse is vast and delicate, and the role you now play within it carries weight."

Evelyn stepped forward, her heart pounding. "We want to learn," she said, her voice clear. "We know the balance is fragile, and we don't take this lightly. Please, teach us how to protect it—and ourselves."

The Guardians began to share their insights, their words weaving together a picture of the multiverse that was as humbling as it was inspiring. They spoke of the connections that bound all realms together, the importance of maintaining harmony, and the dangers of hubris.

The crowd listened in rapt silence, some taking furious notes while others simply stared in awe. Evelyn felt a deep warmth in her chest, a quiet reassurance that they were on the right path.

But then, one man near the back raised his hand. "So, uh," he began, scratching his head awkwardly, "does this mean we're, like, cosmic interns now? Or do we get promoted to full-time Guardians at some point?"

The Guardian of Darkness, who had been silent until now, let out a low chuckle. "Your journey has only just begun," he said, his voice like a distant thunderstorm. "Do not rush to claim titles. Mastery lies in patience."

"Cosmic interns," Evelyn muttered under her breath, shaking her head with a small smile.

As the ceremony came to a close, Liora stepped forward once more. "You have proven your willingness to grow, to reach beyond what is known. But remember, your strength lies in your unity. Protect it, nurture it, and you will accomplish far more than you can imagine."

With that, the Guardians began to fade, their light dissolving into the night sky. The crowd stood in stunned silence for a moment, then erupted into cheers and applause.

Evelyn let out a breath she hadn't realized she was holding, her body sagging with both relief and exhilaration.

Eleven

Chapter 11

E velyn jolted awake, her heart racing. Her eyes darted to the clock on her bedside table—it read 5:48 a.m. She sat up slowly, her mind spinning.

Was it all a dream? she thought, rubbing her temples. The Guardians, Liora, the journeys through dimensions—it had felt so vivid, so real. But now, as she sat in her small, familiar bedroom, it all seemed impossibly far away.

With a heavy sigh, Evelyn swung her legs over the edge of the bed. "It was just a dream," she muttered, disappointment washing over her. "An elaborate, mind-blowing dream."

She stood and stretched, the weight of ordinary life settling back onto her shoulders. "How do I even go back to normal after something like that?" she wondered aloud. The memories felt so clear, so… transformative.

But normal life called, as it always did. Resigned, she shuffled toward the bathroom to start her day.

The guardian veil

Evelyn flipped on the bathroom light and looked in the mirror, ready to face the mundanity of her reflection. But what she saw made her freeze.

It wasn't her reflection staring back.

It was Liora.

Evelyn gasped, stumbling backward slightly. The shimmering figure of the Guardian stood within the glass, her radiant wings glowing faintly, her eyes warm and wise.

"It was real," Evelyn whispered, her voice barely audible.

"Yes," Liora replied, her voice calm and steady. "You have been given a gift, Evelyn—one very few humans ever receive. What you experienced was no child's play. It was a glimpse of the truth, and now it is your path to follow."

Liora's voice softened but carried the weight of infinite understanding. "It was not just a dream, Evelyn," she said, her form glowing brighter in the mirror's reflection. "What you experienced was a *conscious dream*. A projection of your soul into the astral plane. It is a rare gift, and it comes only to those ready to awaken to their greater purpose."

Evelyn's heart pounded in her chest. "Astral plane? You mean... like out-of-body experiences?"

Liora nodded, her shimmering form gently shifting as if she were part of the light itself. "Exactly. While your physical body slept, your consciousness traveled. You were not bound by the limits of your world or your body. That is why it felt so vivid—because it *was* real."

Evelyn gripped the edge of the sink, her mind racing. "So everything I saw—the dimensions, the Guardians—it actually happened?"

"Yes," Liora said, her gaze steady and reassuring. "Your

Chapter 11

awareness moved beyond the Veil, allowing you to see and experience truths that most cannot. The multiverse is vast and intricate, Evelyn, and you have only glimpsed its edges. But now you must decide how to use what you have learned."

Evelyn took a deep breath, her fingers trembling slightly as she leaned closer to the mirror. "Why me?" she asked. "Why was I chosen for this?"

Liora's expression softened, her glowing wings shimmering with faint streaks of gold. "You were not *chosen* in the way you think," she explained. "This ability is part of who you are—who you've always been. For some, this connection remains dormant, never realized. But your curiosity, your determination, and your willingness to see beyond the surface awakened it."

Evelyn's thoughts churned. It felt like too much, too fast, and yet it made sense in a strange, undeniable way. "So, what happens now? Do I just keep... projecting myself into the astral plane?"

"Not yet," Liora replied. "Astral projection is a powerful tool, but it must be used with intention and care. Your conscious dreams will come when you are ready, when the multiverse calls for you to act. For now, your task is to prepare—learn to ground yourself in both worlds, to balance your physical and astral experiences."

Evelyn frowned. "Balance? What does that even look like?"

"It means staying connected to your world while embracing the knowledge of others," Liora explained. "You have a foot in both realms now, Evelyn. Use your gifts to guide and inspire, but do not lose yourself in the process. The line between awareness and overwhelm is thin, and your strength will come from walking it."

Evelyn let Liora's words sink in, her mind a swirl of possibilities and doubts. "Okay," she said finally, her voice steadier than she expected. "So… what do I do next? Like, today?"

A faint smile curved Liora's lips. "Today, you live. The answers you seek will come in time. Trust your intuition, follow the sparks of connection you feel, and remain open to what the world shows you. Every choice you make shapes the balance, Evelyn. Every small action matters."

Evelyn stared at the mirror, her reflection slowly returning as Liora's form began to fade. "Wait!" she said quickly. "Will I see you again?"

Liora's voice echoed softly, even as her image disappeared. "I am always with you, Evelyn. In the light, in the dreams, and in the moments of clarity that guide you. Trust yourself. The journey has only begun."

As the bathroom fell silent, Evelyn stared at her own reflection, her chest rising and falling as she tried to process everything. It wasn't a dream, and it wasn't just her imagination. She had touched something vast, something that changed everything.

Evelyn straightened, a small smile forming as determination bloomed within her. This wasn't the end of the story—it was the beginning.

She glanced at Nimbus, who had wandered into the doorway, his golden eyes fixed on her as if he somehow understood. "Looks like we've got some work to do, Nim," she said, scratching his head.

Nimbus purred in agreement.

And as Evelyn stepped out of the bathroom, a spark of excitement lit within her. Life as she knew it might never be the same—but she wouldn't have it any other way.

Made in the USA
Columbia, SC
03 February 2025